Together at Christmas

Eileen Spinelli

illustrated by **Bin Lee**

Albert Whitman & Company
Chicago, Illinois

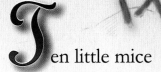en little mice

huddled in the snow

on Christmas Eve.

One scoots below

a broken branch of moonlit pine.

One mouse warm. Now there are nine.

Nine little mice in the frosty dark.

One mouse takes a strip of bark

to make a tent against the chill.

Eight little mice, shivering still.

One mouse spies a wisp of red—

a feather for a feather bed!

Down she cuddles. Ahhh . . . that's nice.

Seven little mice, still cold as ice.

One mouse quickly flits across

the field to where a clump of moss

is pillow-soft. He's safe and sound.

Six little mice crouch on the ground.

One mouse finds a fallen nest.

Room enough for one to rest.

Gratefully, she nestles there.

Five little mice hunched down where

December's wind is sharp indeed.

One mouse sees a toppled weed—

a milkweed pod. A comfy space.

How lucky to have found a place!

Four little mice. Freezing night.

One mouse runs to something bright—

two shiny stones atop some twigs.

Add a roof of holly sprigs.

Three little mice in the snowy squall.

One mouse blown beyond the wall

into an acorn shell—*ker-plop*!

A cozy oak leaf drifts on top.

Two little mice, shaking and wet,

haven't found a refuge yet.

One mouse notices a puff—

a gentle burst of cattail fluff.

Quick! Before it starts to float,

he weaves himself an overcoat.

One little mouse in the bitter sleet,

slushy puddles at her feet.

Soon she gives a happy clap.

She's found an upturned mushroom cap.

It cradles her against the storm.

Now all ten little mice are warm.

Though every mouse is snug alone

on feather bed, in nest, by stone—

somehow it doesn't feel quite right

to be without one's friends *this* night.

So . . .

ten lonely mice brave the weather—

out from their shelters. Back together.

Singing carols in the snow.

Giggling under mistletoe.

One mouse squints through patchy fog,

races to a hollow log—

stash of berries, webs homespun,

and best . . .

there's room for everyone!

Merry Christmas!

For the Savages and the Brenners—E.S.

To all of the North American readers.—B.L.

Library of Congress Cataloging-in-Publication Data

Spinelli, Eileen.
Together at Christmas / by Eileen Spinelli; illustrated by Bin Lee.
p. cm.
Summary: Ten little mice, huddled together in Christmas snow, go off one by
one to find warm places to sleep, but soon decide they would rather be together
celebrating the special night. ISBN 978-0-8075-8010-3 (hardcover)
[1. Stories in rhyme. 2. Mice—Fiction. 3. Cold—Fiction.
4.Christmas—Fiction. 5. Counting] I. Lee, Bin, ill. II. Title.
PZ8.3.S759Tog 2012
[E]—dc23
2011036075

Text copyright © 2012 by Eileen Spinelli.
Illustrations copyright © 2012 by Bin Lee.
Published in 2012 by Albert Whitman & Company.

10 9 8 7 6 5 4 3 2 BP 16 15 14 13 12

The design is by Nick Tiemersma.

For more information about Albert Whitman & Company,
please visit our Web site at www.albertwhitman.com.